Where Is Blue and Other Stories

PAGE PUBLISHING, INC.
Conneaut Lake, PA

First originally published by Page Publishing 2021

ISBN 978-1-6624-1303-2 (pbk)
ISBN 978-1-6624-1304-9 (digital)

Printed in the United States of America

Where Is Blue and Other Stories

Shirley E. Wynn

Where Is Blue

We were going to the farm market to buy food and supplies. While we were there, I noticed a man giving puppies away! I asked my mom, "Please, please, Mom, can I have one." She was reluctant at first, but she realized I needed a friend. She let me pick one. I named him Blue. I was so happy! When we got home, Blue slipped out of my hands and ran off to explore his new home.

I ran after him. I could hear him kinda far away, but I kept looking for him, and I followed his barking. I ran into the meadow behind the house thinking that his excited barking might mean he has scared up a critter, like a rabbit or squirrel and was enjoying the chase. He was gone when I got there, so I kept calling and looking I even went to farmer Brown's up the road, but he said he had not seen a new dog in the area. So with a sad feeling in my heart, I went slowly home; and when I came around the corner, I could hear barking and excitement. And then a big smile spread across my face because Blue was there! I ran up and bent down to give Blue a big kiss and hug! I was so happy my friend had been found safe. I love you, Blue.

Three Little Angels

This is a story about three little angels. The first angel is Morning Glory. She tries to help people or animals in difficult situations.

The First Angel

My name is Brayoina, I am a third grader. There's a lot of kids in my class, and sometimes it's not fun to go to school. There is a girl who likes to be mean to me and to a few other kids. They call her Bellene. She's outright mean and hurtful. We get really scared.

One day when we were worrying about what might happen, we heard a voice, but we didn't see anybody. The voice told us not to be afraid; she would help. As time went, Bellene decided she was going to scare us and make sure that we were so frightened, that we could fall and get hurt. And then Morning Glory came from nowhere and made Bellene's plans backfire. Bellene couldn't understand how her plans had failed. But when you do bad things to others, you need help from an angel to make all things right.

The Second Angel

The second angel is Tulip. She tries to help wherever help is needed. I was walking one day, and I noticed a dog that was tied up and didn't appear to have proper space for exercise and no water or food. This was not good, and then Tulip said, "Don't worry, we will take care of this." So Tulip got the attention of the Humane Society, and they spoke with the owner, and they informed him that he had to take care of his pet better. They would be back to check up on him. Any more attention brought to them, they would be back and possibly place the pet in a better home.

Tulip would like to give you some good tips for being a good pet owner!

WATER   FOOD

Anyone who wishes to own an animal (pet), they need to know how to take care of them and be responsible for that pet. A few things to remember:

1. Get them checked out at the vet and make sure they have all their shots.
2. Make sure they have an area to get plenty of exercise.
3. Always make sure they have plenty of water. Check it often especially on hot days.
4. Make sure they have enough food, a good nutritional bag of dog or cat food. Or any pet you may have, this also applies to them.

Tulip says these are some of the ways you can consider yourself a responsible pet owner.

And a whole lot of *love* and *care* for a winning combination for success!

The Third Angel

The third angel is Dragon Lilly. She helps little children who have a hard time living one day at a time. It was a pleasant day. The sun was shining, and it was a lovely spring day. Sometimes that's not enough. If, for some reason, either the father or mother get in a bad mood because something just doesn't go right for them, the children usually take the brunt or whatever, and that is not good. So Dragon Lilly decided enough was enough. She got a message to the authorities, and they came and saved the children from one less bad memory.

My Barnyard Friends

My name is Toby. Would you like to meet my friends? Here is Goosey Loucy. She is a big mother goose, and she has five goslings. She is a good mother! Then we will visit with Chausey. He is a very young male colt. He's got a lot of frisky energy, and he's a lot of fun to watch!

Then we will visit Pearl. She is a big white rabbit, and she is ever so lovely and very lovable. We like to take turns holding her. Then we will put her down for quiet time so she gets her rest. We have a pet squirrel, and his name is Filbert. We love to watch him because he's very cautious and kinda looks funny when he's observing his surroundings to make sure all is safe for him to catch lunch! It's a lot of fun watching him. We also have a cow. Her name is Pinkie because her nose is pink. She is a gentle animal and never caused any trouble. She gives us enough milk so we can have milk with our meals.

I am so happy you enjoyed my barnyard friends.

A Fairy-Tale Adventure

The Little People

"Sid, come out and help us unload the car," Mom had yelled at the young lad, but Sid was daydreaming, and it took longer for him to realize he was wanted to help. His mom was very upset, and Sid felt bad. He turned and just started walking to the woods. He walked and walked with his head down, feeling bad about not being there to help.

Then out of the corner of his eye, he noticed something strange and different. He saw a light flickering in the distance. And as he watched, the base of the tree opened, and a small carriage with a little carriage driver and miniature horses pulling the carriage came out. Sid came up and seemed like a giant to the little people.

The little people could speak, but you had to really listen because they talked softly. Sid asked them where they were from, and they said the Hidden Valley. He asked if they could show him. At first, the little people were leery, but Sid assured them he would not hurt them. The little man waved his hand, and Sid became little like them. The next thing Sid knew, he was in front of a beautiful place, a well-kept home. This was Dr. Armond D. Chantiss's home. Everything was well kept, with beautiful gardens, fountains with miniature statues (frogs, fairies, turtles, lions), and a very nice beautiful pond with goldfish swimming in it. It was a grand place.

The man took Sid to the nice home and introduced him to Dr. Chantiss. They didn't have much company, so he was invited to an evening of great fun. They had ice skates and a nice big pond to skate on. They also had sleds and a lovely hill to slide down on. They had a big bonfire where they could keep warm and have hot apple cider and cookies. They played and played 'til late, and they didn't want it to end, but all good things do.

The little man took Sid back to where they had gotten him. The next thing Sid knew, he was waking up cold, and he thought that was a beautiful dream, and his spirits were lifted.

When he got home, he was happy. His mom was happy to see him. Then he said to his mom, "I'm sorry I was not quick enough to help. I will try to do better."

About the Author

Shirley E. Wynn loves children and would like to help them realize they are special, and they can do whatever they want to, or set their minds to.

Shirley loves to read mystery books, enjoys baking, some cooking, and some gardening. She also loves Country Music and some rock. She has a very tender spot in her heart for animals. She has Snuggles and Sam they can be most amusing to watch. They give us a lot of happiness!

CPSIA information can be obtained
at www.ICGtesting.com
Printed in the USA
BVHW021111120421
604738BV00014B/1870